MAJOR
World Cities

MOSCOW

Mason Crest
450 Parkway Drive, Suite D
Broomall, PA 19008
www.masoncrest.com
Developed and produced by Mason Crest

Printed and bound in the United States of America.

First printing
9 8 7 6 5 4 3 2 1

Series ISBN: 978-1-4222-3538-6
ISBN: 978-1-4222-3542-3
ebook ISBN: 978-1-4222-8362-2

Library of Congress Cataloging-in-Publication Data is on file with the publisher.

Additional images

AA Photo Library: 15bl, 18b, 32b. AKG London: 40t, /Tretyakov Gallery, Moscow 9t, 36t. Associated Press Picture Library: 21b, 25b. Bridgeman Art Library London/New York: /Private Collection/Novosti 10t, 18t, /Tretyakov Gallery, Moscow 32t, 36b, 40b. Jean-Loup Charmet: 9b. Eye Ubiquitous/Featurescapes 26b, /Gary Trotter 12b, /James Davis Travel Photography 5cr, 28t, 29t, 31t. Robert Harding Picture Library: 4, 15rc, 20b, 22, 24b, 28b, 34t, 37b. David King Collection: 24t. Novosti (London): cover, title page, 5bl, 8b, 8t, 10b, 11b, 11t , 14, 19l, 20t, 23t, 27t, 33t, 38t, 39t, 39b, 41c. Rex Features: cover, 12t, 21t, 26t, 27b, 38b, 41b. TRIP: 13t, 15tl, 16, 17tl, 17bl, 17tr, 19r, 23bl, 30b, 30t, 34b, 35t, 37t, 41t. Dreamstime: Sattarm 5, 12; Evmenov Gennadii 13; Arthit Somsakul 17; Reticent 19; Dmitry Trubitsyn 20t; Nikolay Sachkov 20b; Demerzl21 23cr; Juliasha 25t; Gennadiy Petuhov 25b; Olgavolodina 27b; Artzzz 29b; Vladimir Zhuravlev 31b; Sukhova2013 33b; Pavel Losevsky 35b; Elina 37b; Andrey Emelyanenko 42t; Zoom-zoom 42b;Pavel Bachurin 43t; Palinchak 43b.

Words in **bold** are explained in the glossary on pages 46 and 47.

MAJOR
World Cities

BEIJING

BERLIN

LONDON

MOSCOW

NEW YORK

PARIS

ROME

SYDNEY

CONTENTS

Moscow is the capital and largest city of the world's largest country–Russia. This vast nation extends for some 5,592 miles (9,000 km) across two continents,

from Europe in the west to Asia in the east. Moscow is on the flat plain of European Russia and covers 970 square miles (2,511 square km). Its population of about 12.2 million makes it one of the largest cities in the world. The map on the left shows the city of Moscow as well as the Moscow region (in yellow).

The Kremlin's walls, ▲ towers, and buildings are in the foreground of this Moscow view. In the distance are the high-rise buildings where many ordinary Muscovites live.

Circular layout

The city of Moscow, known in Russian as *Moskva,* began as a small settlement on the banks of the Moskva River and gradually expanded. At its heart are the Kremlin, a huge walled enclosure containing many magnificent buildings, and the wide open spaces of Red Square. Beyond this central area, highways and railroads divide the city into five great circles, linked by smaller roads.

MOSCOW

STATUS
Capital of Russia and of the Moscow region

AREA
970 square miles (2,511 square km)

POPULATION
12,200,000 (2015)

GOVERNING BODY
Council led by a mayor

CLIMATE
Temperatures average 66 to 97°F (19 to 36°C) in summer and 9 to -20°F (−13 to −29°C) in winter

TIME ZONE
Greenwich Mean Time plus 3 hours

CURRENCY
1 ruble = 100 kopeks

OFFICIAL LANGUAGE
Russian, written in the **Cyrillic alphabet**

Federal city

The official name of Russia is the Russian Federation, because it has a **federal** form of government. This means that each of its 85 **republics,** regions, and other political units has its own government and also takes part in the national government. Moscow is one of only three cities among the 85 members.

Moscow government

Moscow has a council with as much power as the government of a republic. The city is divided into 12 districts, and each elects its own council members. The whole city votes for a mayor, who is the leader of Moscow's government.

◄ The marble-covered Beliy Dom (White House), where the Russian parliament meets regularly.

Capital city

As Moscow is Russia's capital, it is the place where the national government is based. It is also capital of the 18,148-square-mile (29,206-square km) Moscow region (see map), so the regional governor and administration are housed there.

◄ Russian president Vladimir Putin (center) talks with his defense minister at a Victory Day event, an annual celebration that marks Germany's defeat in World War II.

MAP OF THE CITY

This map shows central Moscow as it looks today. Many of the places mentioned in the book are marked. The inset map gives a closer view of the Kremlin and Red Square.

CENTRAL MOSCOW

SADOVOYE (GARDEN) RING

BOULEVARD RING

see inset

MOSKVA RIVER

1 Gorky Park
2 New Moscow University
3 Beliy Dom
4 Ministry of Foreign Affairs
5 Chekhov House Museum
6 Gorky House Museum
7 Bolshoi Theater
8 Old Moscow University

9 Pushkin Museum of Fine Arts
10 Cathedral of Christ the Savior
11 Tretyakov Gallery
12 Andronikov Monastery and
    Rublev Art Museum
13 Moscow Art Theater
14 Lubyanka
15 Moscow Conservatory

16 Lenkom Theater
17 Central Children's Theater
18 Obraztsov Puppet Theater
19 Old Circus
20 New Circus
21 St. Petersburg Vokzal
22 Sparrow Hills
23 Church of the Great Ascension

THE KREMLIN AND RED SQUARE

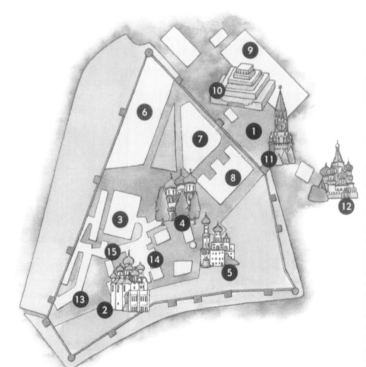

1 Red Square
2 Cathedral of the Annunciation
3 Palace of Congresses
4 Cathedral of the Assumption
5 Ivan the Great Bell Tower
6 Arsenal
7 Senate
8 Presidium

9 GUM
10 Lenin Mausoleum
11 Savior Tower
12 St. Basil's Cathedral
13 State Armoury
14 Palace of Facets
15 Terem Palace

The first Russian **state,** known as Kievan Rus, was set up in the ninth century A.D. By the twelfth century it was divided into **principalities.** Moscow began as a small settlement in a principality called Suzdal. No one is quite sure when this was, though the first known record of the name Moscow dates from 1147. In 1156 the ruler of Suzdal, Prince Yury Dolgorukiy, built a wooden fort in Moscow with a wall around it. This was the original Kremlin.

This modern painting ➤ shows the Kremlin and its surrounding wooden wall in the fourteenth century.

THE TWO-HEADED EAGLE

The **emblem** of Russia is a two-headed eagle. It dates back many hundreds of years. A single eagle was the symbol of the emperors of Rome. When the **Roman Empire** ended in the fifth century A.D., it was followed by the **Byzantine Empire.** This empire lasted until 1453 and adopted a two-headed eagle as its emblem. Moscow had trading links with the Byzantine Empire, and **Czar** Ivan III later married the niece of the last Byzantine emperor. Ivan III decided to take the two-headed eagle symbol to represent Muscovy. Later it became the emblem of all Russia.

Muscovy

Moscow's position on the Moskva River allowed **merchants** to reach it easily from other rivers, so it grew into an important trading center. Then in 1237 the **Mongols,** a warlike people from Central Asia, attacked the city and burned it down. The city was rebuilt, but for more than 200 years had to pay **tribute** to the Mongols. In 1263 Moscow became a separate principality called Muscovy, with its own ruler, Prince Daniil. He and his successors expanded Muscovy by conquering other principalities.

Expansion

In 1380 the Russians defeated the Mongols at the Battle of Kulikovo Field. In 1480 Prince Ivan III (Ivan the Great) refused to make any more payments to them and ended their power in Russia. He also made Muscovy the largest state in Europe and extended the Kremlin. Ivan IV (Ivan the Terrible) expanded Muscovy still further during his reign (1533–84).

Czar Ivan IV earned his nickname ▲ "the Terrible" by killing thousands of people, including one of his sons.

▲ This sixteenth-century map shows two rivers in Moscow, the Moskva and the Neglinnaya. Now the latter runs underground.

A new capital

Rival czars fought in Moscow in the early 1600s; then in 1613 the Romanov **dynasty** took over. Peter the Great came to power in 1689 and changed the nation's name from Muscovy to Russia. He felt Moscow was out of touch with modern Europe, so he built the city of St. Petersburg on the shores of the Baltic Sea, facing Western Europe. In 1712 this new city became Russia's capital.

Moscow continued to grow and prosper in the eighteenth century, even though it was no longer Russia's capital. Business people set up factories there, and the population steadily increased (see page 24). But there were setbacks. Fires raged through the streets in 1737, 1748, and 1752. Then, in 1771, plague struck, and more than 57,000 people died.

Napoleon Bonaparte

In 1812 the French ruler Napoleon Bonaparte invaded Russia. In September the two sides fought the Battle of Borodino near Moscow. Neither side won, but the Russian commander ordered everyone to leave the city. Napoleon's troops moved in to occupy Moscow, but then fire broke out. It burned for six days and destroyed 6,496 houses and 122 churches. The French soon retreated, and the following year the Russians began to rebuild their city.

Russian troops at the Battle of ▲ Borodino. About 70,000 French and Russian soldiers were killed.

Revolution

By 1900 Moscow's industry had expanded, but factory workers were poor and badly treated. They began to protest about conditions, and in 1905 **revolution** broke out in St. Petersburg and Moscow. It was crushed, but in 1917 the **Russian Revolution** began, and a **Communist** government led by Vladimir Lenin took over. In 1918 Moscow became Russia's capital again, and in 1922 Russia joined the Union of Soviet Socialist Republics (USSR).

◄ Communist soldiers defended their Moscow headquarters during the Russian Revolution of 1917. Fighting in the city lasted ten days.

Wartime

In June 1941, during World War II, German troops invaded the USSR. They came within about 20 miles of Moscow, but the city was successfully defended. After the war the USSR and other Communist countries opposed Western **capitalist** countries such as the United States and Great Britain, during a period known as the **Cold War.**

▼ Celebrations marked Moscow's 850th anniversary in 1997.

▲ Joseph Stalin ruled the USSR from 1928 to 1953. He was an ambitious man and ruthlessly killed all opponents (see page 27).

The Russian Federation

In 1985 Mikhail Gorbachev came to power in the USSR and began to make its government more **democratic.** He also increased contacts with capitalist countries, and in 1991 the Cold War officially ended. In August 1991, Gorbachev's opponents led a **coup** against him. He survived, but the USSR collapsed in December. Russia, the largest and most powerful of its 15 republics, became the Russian Federation, with Moscow as its capital. The new leader, Boris Yeltsin, continued Gorbachev's reforms. The current president is Vladimir Putin, who began his second tenure in 2012. His first was from 1999–2008.

People of about 100 different nationalities live in Moscow. Most are Russians, but there are also many people from **republics** that were once part of the USSR, particularly the Ukraine, Belarus, and Armenia. There are also many Tatars, descendants of the Mongols who invaded Russia in the thirteenth century (see page 9). Moscow has a large Jewish community, too.

▲ Thousands of Russia's 6 million Tatars live in Moscow. Most of the rest, like these women, live in the republic of Tatarstan, to the south.

Here's a living room of one of ▼ Moscow's wealthiest, though few people in the city can live like this.

A growing population

Since World War II the number of people in Moscow has risen steadily. In the past 45 years, it has grown by more than 5 million to about 12 million (see page 5). Most of the city's new inhabitants moved there from the countryside in the hope of finding factory, office, or shop work. Many have not settled in central Moscow, but in suburbs such as Babushkin, where new industries provide jobs.

Wealth and power

There is a huge division between rich and poor in modern Moscow. Now that there is more economic freedom, a few fortunate businesspeople have grown rich. On a 2013 list of the world's richest people, Moscow had more billionaires (76) than any other city in the world.

Economic Growth

Moscow's economy fought through hard times in a period of change, and the city now has one of the largest economies in Europe. It accounts for more than one-fifth of the total value of goods and services produced in Russia. Almost everyone of working age in Moscow has a job (the unemployment rate as of the 2010 Census was just 1 percent), and the average Muscovite earns a monthly wage that is almost twice the national average, although Moscow's cost of living is high.

▲ The interior of a huge shopping mall in Moscow.

The rise of racism

The collapse of the USSR had another serious effect on Moscow's people. As republics became independent, they each wanted to rebuild their national identity. Russia tried to do the same, but some people took this too far and became extreme **nationalists.** They believe that only Russian people should be allowed to live in Russia. Many non-Russians in Moscow, especially **Gypsies** and people from former **Soviet** republics such as Georgia and Azerbaijan, suffered racist attacks. Jewish communities also have been victims of anti-Semitism.

WESTERNIZATION

Many Muscovites are adopting aspects of Western European and American culture. Those with enough money can eat in Pizza Hut or McDonald's and buy Adidas sportswear or American-style jeans (right). They can even watch English-language films and bands. Young people in particular are making the most of these new opportunities, but many older people are clinging to their traditional ways of life.

Moscow's earliest buildings were made of wood. In the thirteenth century Prince Daniil (see page 9) ordered the construction of the city's first stone buildings. Since then magnificent structures in a wide variety of styles have grown up in Russia's capital. But many of the greatest and oldest buildings still stand in the heart of the city–the Kremlin and Red Square.

When St. Basil's Cathedral ➤ was completed in 1560, it was white with gold "onion" domes. In the seventeenth century it was painted to create the multicolored building that exists today.

The Kremlin

In 1367, after several disastrous fires, the original wooden walls of the Kremlin were replaced with dazzling white limestone. Ivan III (see page 9) demolished all this to make way for red brick walls and towers encircling 69 acres (27.9 hectares) of land. He also employed Russian and Italian architects to build splendid structures inside the walls. These included the Cathedral of the Assumption, which was used for coronations, and the Cathedral of the Annunciation (right), the private church of the czars.

The Bell Tower

Another important Kremlin landmark is the Ivan the Great Bell Tower. This gold-domed structure was begun in 1505, and reached its present height of 266 feet in 1600. It contains 21 bells, which were rung to warn Muscovites of approaching enemies. The Assumption Bell weighs 72 tons and was tolled three times when a czar died.

Red Square

Red Square runs along the Kremlin's east wall. In the fifteenth century it was a marketplace known as the Burned-Out Site, because fire had once destroyed the area. But by the seventeenth century, attractive buildings stood there, so people called it *Krasnaya* (Beautiful) Square. It is now known as Red Square, because *krasnaya* no longer means "beautiful" but "red." The square is packed with famous landmarks. Among the best known is St. Basil's Cathedral, which was built for Ivan the Terrible. It is now a museum.

▲ Lenin's Mausoleum in Red Square was built in 1930. It contains the **embalmed** body of Vladimir Lenin (see page 10).

This stunning building is the Cathedral ▼ of the Annunciation. Its nine domes were covered in gold on the orders of Ivan IV.

STALINIST ARCHITECTURE

Joseph Stalin (see page 11) wanted to make Moscow the ideal Communist capital, so he set up a committee to decide how to do this. As a result of the committee's plans, seven skyscrapers were built. These included the 564-foot-high Ministry of Foreign Affairs (above) and the 790-foot-high Moscow University, at one time the tallest skyscraper in the city (see pages 20-21). The skyscrapers are sometimes known as wedding-cake palaces.

To escape from the hustle and bustle of city life, many Muscovites head for the green areas beyond the city border. Here, in a zone covering about 695 square miles (1,118 square km), are oak, pine, fir, and birch woods, grassy meadows, and winding streams. Moscow itself also has parks and gardens where citizens can rest and play.

Gorky Park

Gorky Park is on the right bank of the Moskva River, just outside the Sadovoye (Garden) Ring. The park covers 598 acres (242 hectares) and was founded in 1928 as the first Communist Park of Culture and Rest. Russians who visited it had to listen to political speeches, too. Loudspeakers boomed across the park from the government buildings in the Kremlin.

◄ A Ferris wheel towers over one of Gorky Park's lakes. The park is named after the Russian writer Maxim Gorky.

The modern park

Today Gorky Park is very different. Muscovites young and old flock to its fun fairs, boating lakes, open-air theater, and skating rink. Others stroll along the river or admire the ornamental gardens. Thousands of people visit the ice sculptures that are displayed every February.

Izmaylovsky Park

Moscow's 815-acre (330-hectare) Izmaylovsky Park (right) lies to the east of the city. The park was named after the Izmaylov family, its original owners. In the sixteenth century it was bought by the Romanovs, who became Russia's ruling dynasty (see page 9). They built a cathedral and other buildings on an island in the park. Today the park has cafés, a playground, and sports facilities. It leads into the Izmaylovsky Forest Park, a huge, wooded area where czars used to hunt.

MOSCOW ZOO

The Moscow Zoo is in the west of the city. It was established in 1864 and taken over by the government in 1919. Today the zoo contains more than 6,500 animals, such as this llama (left), and attracts well over one million visitors every year. The zoo's entrance is in the shape of a large rock castle, and recent expansions have included an aquarium, an aviary, and a sea-lion exhibit.

A beautiful footpath in one of ▼ Moscow's several botanical gardens.

The Botanical Gardens

There are five Botanical Gardens in Moscow, including the 890-acre (360-hectare) Russian Academy of Sciences' Main Botanical Gardens, located in the northwest part of the city. They were founded in 1945 and include a rose garden that features 2,500 varieties.

◄ The Cathedral of the Intercession stands on the Romanovs' island in Izmaylovsky Park. The cathedral is famous for its tiled exterior.

Early Moscow homes were made of pine and other woods. Carpenters prepared logs in many sizes, and people slotted them together to build anything from a hut to a palace. The logs were numbered to make them easy to assemble, like modern flat-pack furniture.

The Kitai Gorod, east of Red Square, was Moscow's early trading quarter. Many merchants built wooden homes there, as this 1912 painting shows. ▲

Wood and stone

Muscovites first built with stone in the thirteenth century (see pages 14-15), but for 500 years this material was used mainly for public buildings, not houses. From 1714 to 1728, all use of stone in Moscow was banned, as it was needed for St. Petersburg.

Homes of the rich

Wealthy people who did not move to the new capital built many grand homes in Moscow during the eighteenth century. One of the most spectacular was Ostankino, where the palace was made of plaster-covered wood. During the reign of Catherine the Great (1762–96), many stone mansions were constructed in the city for the rich. But when Moscow was rebuilt after its occupation by Napoleon (see page 10), wood was used for most homes. In 1850 half the city's buildings were still made of logs.

◄ Ostankino Palace was owned by Count Nikolai Sheremetev. The count's servants performed plays for his wealthy friends in the palace's beautiful Theater Hall.

Communist construction

Population growth in the late nineteenth century led to a serious housing shortage in Moscow. Apartment buildings were hurriedly built, but most people still lived in overcrowded conditions.

After 1917 the USSR's Communist rulers tried to improve Moscow housing. In the 1950s and 1960s, apartment complexes such as Novyye Cheryomushki were built around the capital. These were owned by the state and divided into apartment groups, each with shops and other facilities. Farther from the city center, taller towers were built, using **prefabricated** concrete sections. The apartments were of poor quality but were cheap, as the state paid most of the rent.

BEYOND THE RING

The Moscow Ring Road was made the city's boundary in 1961, but housing developments soon sprang up beyond it. The most important of these is the new town of Zelenograd (below), to the north of the capital. It was founded in 1963 and is now recognized as one of Moscow's 12 administrative divisions (see page 5).

◄ Most of the people who live in Moscow live in high-rise apartment buildings such as this one.

Housing today

Almost all residents of Moscow live in apartment buildings many stories high. (Largely because of that, Moscow has twice as many elevators as New York City!) There are few single-family homes within the city limits, and extreme traffic makes commuting into the city for work impractical.

Looking ahead

After the Communist era ended, the government began to sell state housing to private owners. It also encouraged housing **cooperatives**, whose members join together to build new homes and renovate old apartment buildings. Still, Moscow's high cost of living is in large part because of rent, and the only townhome communities in the city have only recently been established.

EDUCATION

Every child in Russia must attend school from the age of 7 to 17, with specialized training schools an option for the last two years of the 11-year program. Many begin their education earlier by joining a nursery. Many also continue into higher education at senior school and university.

◄ Russian children at play in a nursery school. Muscovites often begin their education before the official starting age of seven.

Moscow State University

In 1702 Peter the Great set up two of Moscow's earliest centers of learning, the School of Artillery and the School of Navigation. They no longer exist, but Moscow State University, also founded in the eighteenth century, has survived. The university was established in 1755 by scientist Mikhail Lomonosov, and the original buildings near the Kremlin are still used. Most of the university's 37,000 students now attend classes in the Sparrow Hills, southwest of the city center.

Friendship University

Another important institution in Moscow is the Patrice Lumumba People's Friendship University. It was founded in 1960 and provides education for students who come from developing countries in Africa and elsewhere.

Schools for science

Moscow contains many centers for studying science. The most important is the Russian Academy of Sciences. It was founded in St. Petersburg in 1724 but moved to Moscow in 1934. During the Soviet era, members of the Academy of Sciences had to make sure that their research supported Communist ideas. Now they are more free but receive much less money from the government, so they still find it hard to carry out research.

Agriculture

Another Moscow science center is the Timiryazev Agricultural Academy. It was founded in 1865, then in 1923 was named after K. A. Timiryazev, a botanist who taught there. Students from around the world now learn scientific farming techniques there.

Andrei Sakharov was a leading member of ▲ the Academy of Sciences and fought to free it from Soviet control. He won the Nobel Peace Prize (1975) and the Albert Einstein Peace Prize (1988) for his human rights work.

◄ The main building of Moscow State University has 36 stories. The gold star on the top weighs about 12 tons.

MAKING MUSIC

The Moscow Conservatory is the largest music school in Russia and one of the greatest in the world. It was founded in 1866. The famous Russian composer Pyotr Tchaikovsky taught at the school for 12 years

until 1878, which is why it is also known as the Tchaikovsky Conservatory. Every four years the famous International Tchaikovsky Competition for classical musicians is held in the Conservatory's Great Hall. The most-recent competition was held in June of 2015.

Before the 1917 revolution most people in Russia were **Orthodox Christians.** They were members of the Russian Orthodox Church. Muslims, Buddhists, and Jews also lived in the country. Under Communist rule people were not allowed to practice religion, and many religious buildings were closed or used for other purposes, such as restaurants. In 1917 Moscow had 848 churches. By 1990 only 78 were places of worship.

◄ Danilov Monastery is a thirteenth-century group of religious buildings founded by Prince Daniil (see page 9). A holy well stands in front of the monastery.

Communism and the Church

In the 1980s Mikhail Gorbachev (see page 11) began to relax government control over religion as part of his policy of *perestroika* (reconstruction). In 1988 he met Patriarch Pimen, head of the Church, and together they agreed to reopen many churches. Then in 1990 a new law was passed that allowed Russians to follow their religion freely.

Restoration plans

Regular services now take place at about 150 Moscow churches. Kazan Cathedral, demolished by Joseph Stalin in 1936, has been rebuilt on its original site in Red Square. It reopened in 1993. The reconstruction of the Cathedral of Christ the Savior, blown up by Stalin in 1931, was completed in 1998 (see pages 42-43). The total cost was about $300 million.

Prayers are recited ➤
five times every day
at Moscow Cathedral
Mosque. The main
service of the week is
on Friday afternoon.

Moscow mosque

About 75 percent of Russians are Christians. Muslims form the second largest religious group, with about 1.5 million living in Moscow. Many more live outside the city in republics such as Tatarstan. The main place of worship for Moscow Muslims is the Cathedral Mosque. There is also an Islamic Center and the Moscow Muftiyat, a religious organization for Muslims in Moscow and surrounding regions.

NEW RELIGIONS

The 1990 law that allowed Russians freedom of religion also allowed Bibles and other religious literature to be brought into the country once more. It also became easier for foreigners to visit. As a result many new religious groups have arrived in Moscow. These include members of the Hare Krishna sect of Hinduism, as well as **Scientologists.** There were already about 2 million Protestant Christians in Russia, but many more have arrived from other countries hoping to attract people to join their particular group.

The Choral Synagogue is one of the largest in ▼ Moscow and site of important services.

City synagogues

There are now fewer than 100,000 Jews in Moscow. Their numbers have been falling for years because many have emigrated to Israel and elsewhere—as recently as 1989 there were 175,000 Jews in Moscow. Moscow synagogues include the Choral Synagogue, which is the largest in the city. Some Muscovites have strong anti-Jewish feelings, and synagogues have been targeted in bomb and arson attacks.

Russian industry first prospered during the reign of Peter the Great (1689–1725). More than 30 factories were built in Moscow, mostly textile mills producing goods such as army uniforms. Industry continued to grow over the years, providing thousands of jobs.

Communist industry

After the 1917 revolution, the Communist government took over the country's industry. It planned to turn Russia into an industrial giant. Engineering, car, and metalworking industries were developed in Moscow. For years the city's largest factory was the Likhachov Motor Works, which made ZiL limousines for Communist leaders. Steel, oil, and chemical industries were important, too.

КОМСОМОЛ-УДАРНАЯ БРИГАДА ПЯТИЛЕТКИ

Stalin devised **Five-Year Plans** to ▲ improve industry. Posters like this, which shows a 1930s steel factory, encouraged people to work hard for their country.

▼ As Moscow industry grew, the pollution it produced was not controlled. Poisonous fumes still waft over the city today.

Industry today

Many people in modern Moscow still work in the heavy industries of the Communist era, as well as in industries such as printing and electronic engineering, energy production and software development. Moscow is Russia's largest manufacturer of industrial goods.

◄ It is not uncommon today to see trade shows in Moscow, such as this one for the chemical industry.

Economic change

The collapse of Communism led to major changes in Moscow industry. Many companies went bankrupt because they no longer received money from the state. Many others were **privatized.** Since a financial crisis in the late 1990s, however, economic stability has greatly improved, and many of Russia's largest companies are now headquartered in Moscow.

Financial crisis

Russia's new economic system has also led to high **inflation.** As the value of the ruble plunged, prices soared. In 1998 the country's financial crisis worsened, and the International Monetary Fund, an organization that helps major nations to control their currency, stepped in to help.

MONEY AND MARKETS

Moscow is the financial center of Russia. After Communism ended in Russia, private banks opened for the first time. Now there are about 1,100 financial institutions in Russia, with the most important in Moscow. Russia's first post-Communist **stock market** opened in Moscow in 1991. Today, the largest market in Russia is the Moscow Exchange, which was formed in 2011 when two competing markets (the Moscow Interbank Currency Exchange and the Russian Trading System) merged.

CRIME AND PUNISHMENT

Since the fall of Communism, some crimes have increased sharply in Moscow, particularly muggings and **Mafia** violence. The government is working hard to combat these threats.

The secret police force

In the Communist era the ordinary police, known as the *militsiya,* dealt with everyday crimes such as theft. But in 1917 Lenin also set up a secret police force, called the Cheka, which caught and punished people who did not support the government. The secret police force changed its name several times, finally becoming the **KGB** in 1954. Now the KGB has been replaced by the Federal Security Service.

Modern Moscow police

Today the Russian police are the *politsiya*. They work with the Federal Security Service to track down serious villains. They also keep order on the streets, by arresting drunks, for example. In 1989 Mikhail Gorbachev set up an extra force called **OMON.** They often provide crowd control, for example, at soccer matches.

◄ The *politsiya* maintain the peace on the streets of Moscow.

A police officer wearing military-style clothing uses a sniffer dog to search for drugs at a street market. ➤

Theft

Small-scale crime is common in Moscow. Bands of thieves, many of them Gypsies, often steal money and jewelry from pedestrians. Wealthy, well-dressed business people are particularly at risk.

THE LUBYANKA

In March 1918 the Cheka set up its headquarters in a Moscow building on Lubyanka Square. The building (below) became known as the Lubyanka.

In the 1930s the Communist leader Joseph Stalin ordered the secret police to arrest millions of people who did not support the government. Many of these people were imprisoned in the Lubyanka, then tortured and shot.

Crime

Organized crime has increased in Russia over the past several decades. Some estimates say there are up to 50,000 members of the Russian Mafia. They engage in activities such as drug trafficking, gambling, robbery, and murder. The largest Russian Mafia mob is Solntsevskaya Bratva. It has 9,000 or more members. Rival gang members have sometimes killed one another in the streets in deadly turf wars. Despite the growth of the Russian Mafia, however, the overall crime rate in the city of Moscow has fallen steadily in recent years. In 1998 a new law was introduced that gave police greater powers to test suspected drugtakers. And the per-capita murder rate in Moscow declined by almost 75 percent from 2005 to 2014.

The Moskva River winds through central Moscow for about 50 miles (80 km) and provides a quick route across the city. The Volga-Don and other canals link the river to the Baltic, Caspian, and White seas, as well as the Black Sea and its small neighbor the Sea of Azov. Cargo ships sail along this network to inland and coastal ports.

◄ Boats travel along the Moskva River, with the Bell Tower of Ivan the Great and other splendid Kremlin buildings in the background.

River rides

People use the river to get around, especially in the summer. Tourists can take a leisurely ride on a river boat or speed along on one of the *Raketa* (rocket) hydrofoils. Long-distance travelers can also journey by boat, embarking at either the Northern or Southern River Terminal.

THE MAGNIFICENT METRO

The first Moscow Metro station opened in 1935, as part of Stalin's plan for the reconstruction of the city (see page 15). Now there are

more than 150 stations, and about 8 million people use them each day. Unlike the grimy undergrounds of many cities, the Moscow network is clean, efficient, cheap—and beautiful. Stations such as Komsomolskaya (left) even have marble ceilings and huge crystal chandeliers.

The imposing building of ➤
Yaroslavsky Vokzal (right) was
designed by the famous architect
Fyodor Shekhtel (see page 41).

Roaming by rail

Moscow has nine train stations. The first
to open was St. Petersburg Vokzal in 1851.
Today Red Arrow express trains cover
the 400 miles (644 km) to St. Petersburg
in just five hours. Trans-Siberian Railway
trains depart from Yaroslavsky Vokzal,
then travel across Russia to Vladivostok.
Some passengers continue on branch lines
to Mongolia or China.

▲ Moscow, which had the first trolley buses
in Russia, now boasts the largest trolley bus
system in the world.

Cars, buses, and trams

Many people travel by car, and Moscow's
roads can be very busy. There are also many
buses, **trams,** and **trolley buses,** which carry
thousands of Muscovites around from six in
the morning (5:30 for trams) until one o'clock
at night. Passengers buy tickets in advance
from a kiosk or from the driver and insert the
tickets into a machine for punching. Inspectors
check for cheats and fine anyone without a
punched ticket.

Air travel

Moscow has four airports, including Sheremetyevo II
for international flights. It is situated about 20 miles
(32 km) from the city center, so taxis and special
tourist buses bring new arrivals into the capital.

Before the 1917 Russian Revolution, Moscow was a shopper's paradise. Its highlight was the Upper Trading Arcade, a shopping complex that filled one side of Red Square. It had more than 1,000 shops selling goods from all over Russia and beyond. Today the building houses the famous GUM department store, which contains all kinds of shops, both Western and Russian.

Muscovites can buy a huge variety ▲ of breads from street stalls. Some are flavored with poppy or caraway seeds.

▼ Moscow's richest citizens can afford to buy food at Yeliseev's. Poorer people often go there, too, just to stare at the mouth-watering displays.

The Temple of Gluttons

Another Moscow attraction is Yeliseev's food store, nicknamed the Temple of Gluttons. The building was constructed in the eighteenth century as a princess's mansion. In the nineteenth century Grigory Yeliseev bought the house. He opened a luxury grocer's there to rival the store he already owned in St. Petersburg. Wealthy people flocked to the shop to buy exotic fruits, chocolates, fine wines, and other delicacies. Yeliseev's still exists, and its goods are as expensive as ever.

MARKET LIFE

There are many bustling markets in Moscow. Thousands of weekend traders gather at the market in Izmaylovsky Park (see pages 16-17) to sell everything from **icons** to instruments such as **balalaikas** (right). Farmers bring their produce to food markets such as Cheryomushinsky Market. In the past many stalls had only a handful of poor-quality fruits or vegetables to offer. Now crops are more plentiful, and stalls look much more colorful.

◄ A view of the ornate interior of the GUM department store, which features many different shops.

Communist problems

Agriculture and industry did not prosper under Communist rule. As a result food and other goods were in short supply, and some shops contained only empty shelves. The ruble also fell in value, so most people could not afford much.

A new start

Moscow shops slowly came back to life after Russia's economic reforms. Today, there are more stores and more goods to buy than ever before. The main department stores can be found near Red Square, but in many ways Moscow features shopping like any major Western city. Indeed, branches of many Western chains can be found in Moscow.

Before the 1917 revolution wealthy Russians enjoyed lavish meals with many courses. These were often prepared by French chefs, many of whom came to Russia in the eighteenth and nineteenth centuries. Some set up grand restaurants in Moscow. Russian peasants, then as now, lived on simple food such as cabbage soup, rye bread, beets, and potatoes, washed down with rye beer *(kvas)*.

Restaurants in prerevolutionary ▲ Moscow were among the best in the world. The rich ate there in splendor, while outside the poor went hungry.

▲ Cans of caviar, a popular Russian delicacy. The two main types are red caviar (Siberian salmon eggs) and black caviar (sturgeon eggs).

Restaurant revival

After the revolution both dining out and home cooking took a turn for the worse. Food shortages affected rich and poor alike. Restaurants were taken over by the state, which led to dreary decor, slow service, and badly cooked food. Many Russians went hungry, and soup kitchens could be found on Moscow streets. But new restaurants began springing up, too. Some were cooperatives, where several owners put their money together to pay for the building and food.

On the menu

Many Moscow restaurants specialize in Russian food. Russian meals often begin with *zakuski,* a mixture of small dishes such as pancakes *(blini)* with caviar, gherkins, smoked herring, and ham. Cabbage or beet soup *(borshch)* often follows, then a meat stew or roast, or perhaps fish, for example, stuffed carp. *Pelmeni,* Russian-style ravioli, are another favorite, traditionally filled with pork, beef, or elk. Typical desserts are ice cream or fruit pies.

Peter the Great introduced *zakuski* ▲ to Russia in the eighteenth century. This modern zakuski includes salted fish, blinis, and caviar.

TEA AND VODKA

Russians are famous for their love of two very different drinks—tea and vodka. The Mongols (see page 9) first brought tea to Russia. They also introduced the samovar (below), the large urn used to heat water for the tea. Russians drink tea without milk or sugar, but usually eat something sweet with it, such as a spoonful of jam. Vodka ("little water") is a kind of alcohol made from grain or potatoes. It is drunk ice cold, often followed by a bite of rye bread or gherkin.

Southern specialities

Moscow also has restaurants that serve food from other regions of the former USSR, such as the southern republics of Armenia, Azerbaijan, and Georgia. *Shashlyk* (meat kebabs) are a speciality of all three areas. One Azerbaijani dish is *piti* (lamb stew with fruit), while Georgians enjoy chicken *tsatsivi* (chicken in walnut sauce). Armenians serve *amich* (chicken with almonds and apricots).

Fast food

McDonald's arrived in Moscow in 1990 and famously drew long lines of customers at its branch on Pushkin Square. The fast-food chain became so popular that there are now almost 500 McDonald's in Russia.

THEATER AND ENTERTAINMENT

Moscow has hundreds of theaters, cinemas, and night clubs. After the end of the Communist era, their numbers grew fast.

The Bolshoi Theater

Moscow's most famous theater is the Bolshoi (Great). It was founded by an Englishman, Michael Maddox, in 1776. The Bolshoi Theater has staged many ballets and operas. The first performance of Tchaikovsky's ballet *Swan Lake* took place there in 1877. In Communist times the theater was also used for political events, such as the ceremony to mark the USSR's foundation in 1922. The Bolshoi was closed from 2005 to 2011 for a major rebuilding and renovation. It reopened in October 2011 with a concert featuring international performers, as well as the Boshois ballet and opera stars.

▲ The magnificent Bolshoi Theater has five tiers of seating on both sides of the stalls. It can hold more than 2,000 people.

Plays

The best-known theater for drama in Moscow is the Moscow Art Theater (MKhAT), founded in 1898. Several plays by the important Russian dramatist Anton Chekhov were first performed there, for example, *The Cherry Orchard* in 1904. MKhAT still stages serious plays, but they are no longer as popular with the public.

A modern production at the Moscow Art ▲ Theater. The actors are performing a one-act comedy by Chekhov called *The Bear*.

Other theaters

Moscow has more than 60 theaters, including the Lenkom Theater (formerly the Moscow State Theater), where works of many of the most popular Russian writers have been featured. Younger theater-goers can visit the Central Children's Theater and the Obraztsov Puppet Theater.

> ▼ These expert cyclists at a Moscow circus are managing to balance on one wheel and form a chain while speeding around on the ice.

City circuses

Moscow is famous for its circuses, which include traditional acts such as performing animals, as well as clowns and acrobats. The Moscow State Circus, called the Old Circus, began in 1886. In 1971 the New Circus was set up in a 3,400-seat arena in the Sparrow Hills. Tent circuses are also held at Gorky and Izmaylovskiy parks in the summer.

Music and Nightlife

There was little nightlife in Moscow during the Communist regime, but that has changed now. A vibrant nightclub and music scene can be found all over the city. One of the top live-music venues is B2, which also features a pool hall, sushi bar, and disco. There are lots of other smaller places to listen to music, too, with choices ranging from rock to jazz to blues and more.

MUSEUMS AND ART GALLERIES

Moscow has more than 80 museums and art galleries. Many are now improving their facilities to attract growing numbers of tourists who visit the capital.

The Andrei Rublev Museum

The Andrei Rublev Museum of Early Russian Art is in the Andronikov Monastery. Andrei Rublev was a monk at the monastery in the early fifteenth century. He was a skilled **icon**-painter, and some of his works are in the Cathedral of the Annunciation (see pages 14–15). The museum opened in 1960 and has many icons and embroideries. People also visit the site to see the monastery buildings, particularly the Cathedral of the Savior.

The Tretyakov Gallery

Moscow's Tretyakov Gallery was founded by Pavel Tretyakov, a merchant. He began to collect paintings in 1856 and kept them in his mansion. Later he extended his house and opened it to the public. It has now been extended further and contains over 50,000 paintings, from ancient icons to the works of more recent artists such as Valentin Serov.

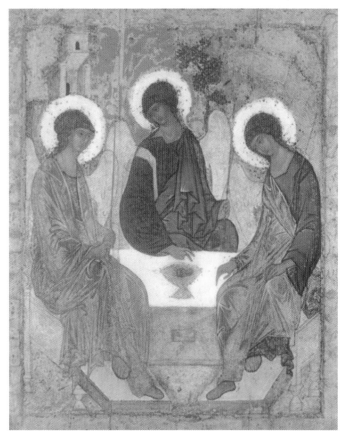

▲ Andrei Rublev painted this icon, *The Old Testament Trinity*, at the Andronikov Monastery. It hangs in the Tretyakov Gallery.

◄ This painting, *Girl with Peaches* by Valentin Serov, is also in the Tretyakov. It shows the daughter of a wealthy Moscow industrialist, Savva Mamontov.

Visitors to Tolstoy's house can view 16 ➤ rooms, including his study (right), where some of his manuscripts are displayed.

The Pushkin Museum of Fine Arts

The Pushkin Museum was founded in 1887 and contains more than 500,000 works. These include Egyptian mummy paintings, Greek vases, Roman statues, and a world-class collection of European paintings by artists such as Botticelli, Rembrandt, and Monet. It also holds many works taken from Germany when the USSR occupied the country after the Second World War.

STATE ARMOURY

The State Armoury in the Kremlin is one of the oldest museums in Moscow. It was established in 1808, but its roots date to the early 1500s, when the building was an arsenal, manufacturing arms and ammunition. Now it contains the magnificent treasures of the czars, such as jewels, crowns, robes, and Catherine the Great's wedding and coronation dresses.

House Museums

The houses of several famous people who lived in Moscow have been turned into museums. The house of playwright Anton Chekhov (see page 34) from 1886 to 1890 is now a museum. Inside, the house looks as it did in Chekhov's time, and visitors can see first editions of his plays.

The Russian novelist Leo Tolstoy spent every winter from 1882 to 1901 in what is now the Tolstoy House Museum. There he wrote the novel *Resurrection* (1899).

Lenin Mausoleum

Also known as Lenin's Tomb, the embalmed body of Soviet leader Vladimir Lenin (see page 10) can still be viewed several days a week. Visitors to the mausoleum are required to show respect, and no photography or video is allowed.

Special events take place all year round in Moscow. Some are serious religious or political occasions; others are festivals designed to be fun for everyone.

The Winter Festival

Moscow's Winter Festival is from December 25 until January 5. It consists of many events, such as parties and concerts. New Year's Day is the highlight. Parents dress as Grandfather Frost or the Snow Maiden to give their children presents.

THE MOSCOW OLYMPICS

In 1980 the Olympic Games were held in Moscow (below). A huge 130-foot-high sports complex was built for the occasion. Its stadium can hold 40,000 people and is now used for major soccer, rugby, ice skating, and athletics competitions.

▲ Women dressed as Snow Maidens dance at a special Christmas show for children in Moscow.

Christmas

Christmas takes place on January 7 for Russian Orthodox Christians. Celebrations were banned in the Communist era but since 1992 have been allowed again. Christians pack Moscow's churches on January 6 and stay overnight at candlelit ceremonies.

Ice festivals

In February, ice-sculpture festivals are held in Gorky Park (see page 16) and elsewhere in the capital. Some people, nicknamed *morzh* (walruses), even break holes in the frozen lake to go swimming.

In the spring

Orthodox Easter occurs in March or April. Muscovites celebrate with special foods such as *kulich,* a yeast cake with almonds and raisins, and *paskha,* a spiced curd cheese cake.

In Communist times a grand military parade was held in Red Square on **May Day** (May 1). This day is still a holiday. Victory Day (May 9) marks Germany's defeat in World War II.

Summer fun

A new Moscow summer celebration is growing in importance, commemorating the day when Russia split away from the USSR (June 12, 1991). It is known as Independence Day and has become a public holiday. Many festivities take place in Red Square and elsewhere. Another summer event is the odd-yearly Moscow Film Festival in July.

▲ Moscow's own festival, the Day of the City, takes place on August 31 each year. Many Muscovites dress up to join in its lively and colorful parades.

Autumn celebrations

Every September the Moscow marathon is run. It begins and ends in Gorky Park. A military procession used to march across Red Square on November 7 every year to commemorate the 1917 revolution. Only a few people still mark the occasion. They stage small marches or take flowers to the Lenin Mausoleum.

◄ This old-style military parade took place in Moscow in November 1982. The placard on the left shows Leonid Brezhnev, who was the ruler of the USSR at the time. He died just three days later.

Moscow has been home to a variety of powerful people through the ages. Some shaped its lands and buildings, and others, its ways of life and thought.

Ivan the Great

Ivan the Great (Ivan III) ruled Moscow from 1462 to 1505. He was tall and handsome and loved to laugh, eat, and drink. But he was also a skillful politician, who made Moscow and the surrounding state of Muscovy a great power. During his reign he conquered rival principalities, freed Muscovy from the Mongols, and increased his own authority. In this way he laid the foundations for Moscow's lasting importance and the czars' immense power.

▲ Ivan the Great built two palaces in the Kremlin. The Palace of Facets contained his throne room, and the Terem Palace was his family home.

▲ Pushkin, shown here in his late 20s, was one of Russia's greatest poets.

Alexander Pushkin

Pushkin was born in Moscow in 1799. He became a writer and was sent away from the city in 1820 because the government disagreed with the political ideas in his poetry. In **exile,** Pushkin wrote the play *Boris Godunov* (1825) and began his verse novel *Eugene Onegin* (1823–31). Pushkin was allowed to return to Moscow in 1826, but the police followed him everywhere. Their records still exist and show that Pushkin lived the high life at literary **salons** and clubs. He was fatally wounded in a duel in 1837. Moscow now has a museum dedicated to his life and work.

Osip Bove

Osip Bove was an architect who redesigned Red Square after the 1812 fire (see page 10). He also created about 500 new buildings. These included the Triumphal Arch to commemorate Russia's victory over Napoleon, and the Church of the Great Ascension, where Pushkin was married.

▲ Mikhail Gorbachev and his wife, Raisa, who died in 1999.

◄ Shekhtel's Gorky House Museum was originally built as a house in 1900. The outside is decorated with ironwork.

Fyodor Shekhtel

Fyodor Shekhtel is another famous Russian architect. He designed many Moscow houses in the **Art Nouveau** style. The best example is the Gorky House Museum, which contains flower-patterned mosaics, colorful stained glass, and a swirling marble staircase.

Mikhail Gorbachev

Gorbachev studied law at Moscow University and graduated in 1955. Thirty years later he became leader of the USSR and introduced the reforms that brought the country to an end in 1991 (see page 11). He has remained active in Russian politics in his post-presidency, as well as working for the Moscow-based Gorbachev Foundation and the Raisa Gorbachev Foundation (named for his wife, who died in 1999), to help children with cancer.

VALENTINA TERESHKOVA

In 1963 Valentina Tereshkova (below) became the first woman in space. In 1994 she took on another high-profile role as head of the Moscow-based Russian Center for International Scientific and Cultural Cooperation. Her job was to build links between scientists in Moscow and those in other countries. She also organizes scholarships for science students and, in 2011, was elected to the Russian legislature.

Moscow has changed enormously since the end of the Communist era. People can vote freely, buy a wider range of goods, even make their fortunes by setting up in business. There are still challenges ahead for the city.

Mighty Moscow

Moscow has managed better than Russia as a whole since the reforms of the 1990s. On average its citizens earn much more than other Russians. Private companies have moved in, and the economy has recovered from a downturn in the 1990s. Government and business leaders have great plans for the future.

◄ The original Cathedral of Christ the Savior took 43 years to build. The new version was completed in just three years. It is now the pride of the city.

Building projects

Offices and shops are springing up all over Moscow. The Moscow International Business Center (MIBC), or Moscow-City, is an enormous undertaking in central Moscow that is being built at an estimated cost of $12 billion. Officials envision a complex in which 250,000 to 300,000 people at any given time are working, living, or being entertained. The project began in the early 1990s. Many portions have been completed, but some are ongoing.

OSTANKINO TOWER

At 1,772 feet (540 m), Ostankino Tower is the tallest freestanding structure in Europe. The television and radio tower was completed in 1967 to mark the 50th anniversary of the October Revolution (see page 11).

Almost all of Russia's nationwide television networks, radio stations, major newspapers, and magazines are headquartered in Moscow.

Reaching for the sky

Federation Tower—actually two skyscrapers built on one podium—was completed in the Moscow International Business Center in 2016. When finished, the 97-story Tower East will be the tallest building in Europe. The Tower West is a 65-story building.

Facing the future

Russia is facing the future—the immediate future at least—with Vladimir Putin as president. A long-time officer in the KGB, Putin became acting president of Russia on the last day of 1999, when Boris Yeltsin resigned. Putin then won elections in 2000, 2004, and 2012 (the latter being a six-year term after a change to Russian law in 2011).

Putin's terms in office have been characterized ▲ by economic growth and gains in areas such as energy and high-tech industry, and he has been credited with stabilizing Russia in the post-Soviet era. However, he also has come under intense criticism—including from former Soviet President Mikhail Gorbachev (see page 41)—for moving away from democracy, and for his use of military intervention in areas such as Ukraine.

TIME LINE

This time line shows some of the most important dates in Moscow's history. All the events are mentioned earlier in this book.

NINTH CENTURY A.D.

State of Kievan Rus established

TWELFTH CENTURY

1147

First known record of the name Moscow, taken as date of city's foundation

1156

Prince Yury Dolgorukiy builds first Kremlin

THIRTEENTH CENTURY

1237

Mongols attack Moscow

1263

Principality of Muscovy established

FOURTEENTH CENTURY

1380

Russians defeat Mongols at Battle of Kulikovo Field

FIFTEENTH CENTURY

1462-1505

Reign of Ivan III (the Great)

1480

Ivan III ends tribute payments to Mongols

SIXTEENTH CENTURY

1533-84

Reign of Ivan IV (the Terrible)

SEVENTEENTH CENTURY

1605-13

Rival czars fight in Moscow

1613

Romanov dynasty comes to power

1689-1725

Reign of Peter the Great

EIGHTEENTH CENTURY

1712

St. Petersburg becomes Russia's capital

1755

Moscow University founded

1762-96

Reign of Catherine the Great

1771

Plague kills more than 57,000 in Moscow

1776

Bolshoi Theater founded

NINETEENTH CENTURY

1812

French and Russian troops fight Battle
of Borodino on Moscow's outskirts

1851

First railroad station, St. Petersburg Vokzal,
opens

1864

Moscow Zoopark opens

1866

Moscow Conservatory founded

1873

Tretyakov Gallery opens

1877

Premiere of Tchaikovsky's Swan Lake
at Bolshoi Theater

1886

Moscow State Circus opens

1887

Pushkin Museum of Fine Arts opens

1898

Moscow Art Theater (MKhAT) founded

TWENTIETH CENTURY

1905

Revolution breaks out in St. Petersburg
and spreads to Moscow

1917

The Russian Revolution begins. Czars'
rule ends and a Communist government
is set up under Vladimir Lenin
Cheka secret police formed

1922

Union of Soviet Socialist Republics
(USSR) formed

1928-53

Rule of Joseph Stalin

1928-32

First Five-Year Plan

1931

Cathedral of Christ the Savior demolished

1935

First Moscow Metro station opens

1936

Kazan Cathedral demolished

1941

German troops invade USSR
but are driven back from Moscow

1945-1991

Cold War

1954

KGB formed

1958-64

Rule of party leader Nikita Khrushchev

1963

New town of Zelenograd founded

1977-82

Rule of Leonid Brezhnev

1980

Olympic Games held in Moscow

1985

Mikhail Gorbachev becomes leader of USSR

1990

New law allows freedom of religion
First McDonald's opens in Moscow

1991

Coup against Gorbachev leads to collapse of
USSR and formation of Russian Federation

1997

Moscow celebrates 850th anniversary

1998

Economic and political crisis hits Russia
New Cathedral of Christ the Savior opens
New anti-drug laws introduced

TWENTY-FIRST CENTURY

2000

Vladimir Putin is elected to his first four-year
term as president

2011

The Bolshoi Theater reopens after a major
renovation

2012

Vladimir Putin is elected to six-year term as
president

Art Nouveau   A style of art and architecture that was popular from about 1890 to 1910. It featured swirling shapes and images of natural objects such as plants and leaves.

balalaika   A three-stringed instrument, usually with a triangular body.

Byzantine Empire   The empire founded by the Roman emperor Constantine when he left Rome in A.D. 330. It was based in the old Greek city of Byzantium, which he renamed Constantinople after himself.

capitalist   Relating to capitalism, a system in which businesses are owned by private individuals rather than the state. *Compare Communist.*

Cold War   The time when the USSR and other Communist countries were enemies of the United States and other capitalist countries, but did not fight them in a violent "hot" war. The cold war lasted from about 1945 to 1991.

Communist   Relating to Communism, a system in which businesses are owned by the state, and there is only one political party. *Compare capitalist.*

cooperative   A business that is owned and funded by a group of people, who share its profits.

coup   An attack designed to overthrow a ruler or government.

Cyrillic alphabet   An alphabet based on Greek letters that is used to write Russian. It is named after a ninth-century saint called Cyril, who may have invented it.

czar   The title of the emperors of Russia. It is a form of the word *Caesar,* which was the title of the emperors of Rome.

democratic   Involving all the people, especially by allowing them to elect the leaders who govern them.

dynasty   A family that rules a country for generations.

embalmed   Treated with chemicals to prevent decay.

emblem   An image that symbolizes something, for example, a country.

exile   Absence from one's usual home, normally as a result of being forced to leave.

federal   Relating to a kind of government in which regional and national authorities share power.

Five-Year Plans   A series of plans for economic development in the USSR. The first, introduced by Stalin, lasted from 1928 to 1932.

Greenwich Mean Time   The time in Greenwich, England, which stands on the zero line of longitude.
It is used as a base for calculating the time in the rest of the world.

Gypsies   A nomadic (traveling) people who live in many countries, particularly in Europe. Gypsies are believed to have come from India.

icon   A religious painting. Many icons are painted on wood and decorated with gold.

inflation   An excessive increase in the price of goods.

KGB   The secret police of the USSR from 1954 to 1991. The initials stand for Russian words that mean "Committee of State Security."

Mafia   A secret criminal organization.

May Day   A holiday in honor of work and workers that is held on the first day of May.

merchant   A trader who buys and sells goods to make money.

Mongols   A warlike people who conquered Central Asia in the thirteenth century A.D., led by Genghis Khan.

nationalist   A person who is loyal to and proud of his or her country, sometimes in an extreme way.

OMON   A special police force that deals with problems such as street disturbances and demonstrations. The initials stand for Russian words that mean "workers' police support detachments."

Orthodox Christians   Followers of the beliefs and practices of the Orthodox churches of the East, which split from the Roman Catholic Church of the West in the eleventh century A.D.

prefabricated   Ready-made. Apartment towers are often built with concrete blocks made in a factory and put together on a building site.

principality   An area of land ruled by a prince.

privatized   Sold to private owners.

republic   A country or other political unit with elected rulers and no king or queen.

revolution   A period of unrest and violence during which a government or ruling class is removed from power.

Roman Empire   The vast empire ruled from Rome from 27 B.C. to A.D. 476. At its largest it stretched from Britain to the Caspian Sea.

Russian Revolution   The revolution that took place in Russia in 1917. In the February Revolution the rule of the czars ended, and a Provisional Government was set up. In the October Revolution the government was overthrown, and Communist rule under Vladimir Lenin began.

salon   A meeting of rich, fashionable guests to discuss subjects such as art and literature.

Scientologist   A member of a religion founded in California in 1954. Its members receive therapy to help them deal with bad experiences from the past.

Soviet   Of or relating to the USSR, which was also known as the Soviet Union.

state   A country or other political unit that governs itself and makes its own laws.

stock market   A place where traders buy and sell company shares to make money.

trams   Streetcars that travel on rails and receive power from overhead wires.

tribute   Payment in money, goods, or even people made by one state to another, more powerful state.

trolley buses   Buses that receive power from overhead wires like trams, but which travel on the road, not on special tram rails.

INDEX